Copyright © 1985 Editions Duculot, Paris-Gembloux
Translation copyright © 1986 by William Morrow and Company, Inc.
First published in Belgium under the title *Ernest et Célestine au Musée.*
Printed in Belgium   First American Edition   10 9 8 7 6 5 4 3 2 1

Library of Congress Cataloging-in-Publication Data
Vincent, Gabrielle.   Where Are You, Ernest and Celestine?
Translation of: Ernest et Célestine au musée.
Summary: When Celestine momentarily loses Ernest at the museum,
she fears that he prefers the paintings to her.
[1. Art museums—Fiction. 2. Museums—Fiction.
3. Bears—Fiction. 4. Mice—Fiction] I. Title.
PZ7.V744Wh 1986   [E]   85-17595
ISBN 0-688-06234-2
ISBN 0-688-06235-0 (lib. bdg.)

Where Are You, Ernest and Celestine?

GABRIELLE VINCENT

GREENWILLOW BOOKS
NEW YORK

"Wait, Ernest, look at those big white statues."
"Not now, Celestine. We don't want to be late."

"I can only take the job if Celestine can come with me."
"I don't think that will be possible, but you can ask the director."

"No, I'm afraid you can't bring the child to work every day. But as long as you're here, why don't you both look around and enjoy the museum."

"Look, Ernest, I'd like to do that!"

"It must be nice to work among all these wonderful paintings."
"Yes, it is nice, but sometimes it's a bit too quiet."

"What a lot of pictures!
All right, Celestine, how about
a piggyback ride to the end
of this gallery?"

"Look, Celestine, she smiles
    just the way you sometimes do!"

"We've been here a long time, Ernest. I'm getting tired."

"Just let me look at a few more paintings, Celestine."

"Ernest! Where are you?"

"I've lost Ernest!"
"No, I just saw him.
  He's in the next gallery."

"What shall I do now?"

"The gallery is the other way, my dear.
This is a private office."

"Is that you, Ernest?"
"No, but if you're Celestine, I heard someone calling you."

"If you're Ernest, your little one is here."

"Oh, Celestine, I've looked everywhere for you!"

"Here are the statues you wanted
to see, Celestine."

"I don't want to see anything.
I just want to go home!"

"What's the matter, Celestine?"
"If you change your mind and take the job, I will be alone all day."
"But I'm not taking it, Celestine."

"I was really frightened when I was lost, Ernest."
"But you're not lost now, Celestine."

"I thought you liked the pictures better than me."

"There is nothing I like better than you, Celestine!"
"There is nothing I like better than you, Ernest!"